Island Song

Urban Honolulu Island Ambiences, Seaside and Mythological

MATTHEW KRAUS

ISBN 978-1-965679-20-3 (Paperback)
ISBN 978-1-965679-21-0 (Ebook)

One

"This was not too bad," commented David E. an independent songster of the islands residing and working his craft out of near downtown Honolulu.

When he was younger. It, however, was in many local and local sponsoring happenings or/and singing events.

To his friends, he conversed.

David conceded, "It's not uncommon, and a lot of the people coming to visit the show are sympathetic towards the broad presentation."

He had finished songs; and he was plugging them the best they could, as the show went on.

And as he had a lovely, younger work that represented his time, he had a show that flourished, it survived well enough to get him by. And unexpectedly, it looked like a regular stream of visitors to sample hula dancing was going to be reliable.

The songs were well-taken, some were humorously intended and most could be seen to beckon to other favorites.

Some of a show included a free patron hula experience.

David would supply the hula hoop.

With some basic lessons, and more seriously with a regular adult class, she progressed to hula dance-progressed, he was not a constant street singer musician. She had also held onto some regular performances of the times and was all for getting by acquainted with the, yet, once-more playing at numerous parties and luaus. The performer was a success.

Some backup music of the lovely rural areas that still existed in most parts of the town were home for both David E. and Honey, the hula dancer lady. David, the maverick performer, had memories of growing up familiar with shows, which included times when they were on their own, hiking and going to occasional professional performances.

It was not going out of the way with supporting the many performers. Then, this was the flower-chasing growing up; which, nonetheless, included the experience he had brought to lei giving success, and that was about the many selves who were in enjoyment of it, and to support the show so it worked out well.

At a work site, the performer and dancer were conversing.

Honey clarified, "You mean, we've got another opportunity?"

David answered, "Yes. But she's still selling leis and flowers."

The forgotten lei stand wasn't still in business. Nonetheless, they wanted it to continue on; at least in memory.

David sat about a performance site downtown.

She drove and parked a car nearby to see old friends. One old friend, who would polish the car for her, brought her more flowers than a normal tourist lei, that has to add to the hula site where she had acquired the practice of hula in recent months, mostly through David; and she shared some of the floral blessing with David, sometimes giving him a lei.

It had been quite a while since the lei stand had gone out of business. The lei stand shack, itself, has been sold to a house buyer. They had watched as it was moved to a historic site. But she maintained it had managed to come through, and anyone could continue with it.

The flowers were scenery, and making and selling leis from her home and other places had worked. But her journey was as a background visitor.

As the performance songs were getting in public, she and David were out and about; they had gotten more patrons; more interested in current popular hula dance songs; and they were working on songs, musically. Pretty soon, introducing the songs, these were with aloha, to the many people who stopped by; it was a good one that warmed the heart of performer and listener alike. They were into doing a set of a few original aloha songs. The performances were gaining popularity as aloha themes, and aloha would work, as such, at an opening of a particular set. The opening songs of that there were a few with the aloha word in it, and that went on and on.

David was fluid, sometimes more pro-minded, sometimes successful.

After a while, situated on a grassy area, comfortable about a mall, in line with working the aloha song theme, he grew his performance to a set that lasted long.

"It's been the last ten or twelve months," David commented.

Honey replied, "Now, we've got to dance. So, sing it and get it in my mind." She was helpful as well as talented. Her two hula friends, also would join her and David as time went on, for a somewhat spontaneous permanence spree.

While they had a more professional appearance, they were charitable and gave off their talent to what show David could come up with.

After working with David at his off-street site, momentarily donning professional gear, they would return to their appearances, scheduled, and enjoyable.

The *pupu* (slang, pigeon- appetizers) added to the performance's success. There were often plates and platters being shared among the performers, timely so they could still continue with the fine performance presentation, as well as the numcours guests and walk by patrons, and interested parties that happened by. In some cases, there were fares given to people in back, as well.

A regular fare of poi was often supplied. then, the most enjoyable deserts were often heaped available. sometimes, they would break and share.

"Thanks." David responded.

"That's okay!"

These hula girls often brought a food gift.

She added, "Go ahead."

David went on, "I've been backing you up with the music of most of your songs for a long time; that's Ok, and I'll pick up the key, I've got the good ear, I can play by ear. And you start with a few beats."

"Here goes."

There were a few seconds before she got through the blank time and he went a Capella (just voice). Then he hit a chord; and he held the guitar upright by the neck, and said, "It's better than just plucking."

He was just doing a music set.

A drowned out, fast-speaking of words gave the song's title, and it starts out pretty good.

As some passersby were there, they politely listened. He sang, "You're going to say: aloha."

One person sang out, "A-lo-ha."

It was soon spring again and they were regularly performing. They were starting to become noticed by residents, night club owners, and flower stand patrons, who were standing about.

The days of song-plugging went on.

"Yes. And then we were about to do the whole song," "Well, let's do the whole song over. Now,"

"Okay,"

There were a few pensive moments and then the redecision. "That's alright,"

"OK."

Angered, but letting it go, they said, "We don't need to do it right now,"

David often stipulated, "Please bring some donuts."

"Be glad to."

"Straight from the store?"

"Day old."

"O.k."

"tuna sandwiches?"

"Sure."

"Beef stew and rice?"

"Why not?"

"Sell 'um on the side!"

"O.k."

"Before the show?"

"Sure.

"And I'd like to break and consume some myself. But then, I suppose it's pau hana (finished work) and we're going home."

"Okay."

David often attended a free luau, given by friends of his at a lunch wagon eatery. Here, he enjoyed a welcome without having to contribute his time and energy to entertaining the friend's owners. Here, the lunch wagon poured out plates of Hawaiian food, on paper plates, and served with an eight-ounce fruit punch, a flavored water that was typical of the accompanying food. Here would be poi, *lomi* salmon, haupia, and kalua pig and cabbage on rice; and he would always be welcome, he could stay around and chat with other people who were part of this lunch wagon's support.

There were times when he concentrated on going to the lunch wagon, where he could be sure of taking home some packaged foods to his performance site in the middle of the afternoon.

There were also generous friends, who came to see him as he performed, besides the few hula dancers that had their lunch wagon fare there to share with him.

There were moments with that when they played this game out at the end of their session. They quietly packed up their rhythm machine, a recorded bass on that, folded small speakers, their guitar and ukulele in their hardwood cases, and walked to their old car.

A baseball song he sang could not have rang out truer! But it would have been hard if not impossible to hula to. Honey might, though, choreograph to hula one or two of his other songs.

Driving home this day to their house, the sun was setting early, they remembered the times they had played at the park under a tree in the corner. David was driving Honey somewhere to lunch.

David said, "There was not much talk there that day, that last day we played."

"This is true," Honey added.

The song, which was being performed as it had been performed, was settling midday.

Then, David headed to their home, the flat in an apartment building next to a rooming house. And further from where they usually hung out and played their songs, the car parked.

A few days later they were back together. Honey was talking to David.

The walk back to the house was with discussion.

David commented, "That was pretty good, having the hula dancers come to hula dance."

Honey agreed, "Yes, we got to get them together to hula again?"

"Maybe sometime next week?" David asked. "'I don't think so, David. I've got a date.,"

David sang on in public parks, and other locations of the town; singing on Hawaiian mythological things; hula dancing, Hawaiian language, the surf and sea ambience, and comicall sometimes tunes were the mainstay; also, middle of the road songs loomed into a growing catalog that could overtake just being in the background.

He was someone who had played around at various performance sites.

When he played, sometimes tuning up at a park before going to a location, or about a boulevard, fans came. They usually brought a lei for him, but recently it had been a corsage.

He played on. A performer, he was aware that some of his fans lived nearby. A married couple were loyal; they could often be found coming to visit him. Honey would come again.

His guitar had fans. It had been bought as a gift for him by a fan at an islands' guitar shop. In the late eighteen hundred, the guitar had competed with ukulele in matters of popularity. And though the native Hawaiian instruments had offered some competition, he played ukulele and had manipulated bamboo rattles, he played some mean guitar.

Two

Friends were to come. They came. They were Don Noh and his hula dancing wife-companion, Fanny.

This one time, they were outside on a street corner, waiting for a taxi, which was late to pick them up by a few minutes because of traffic. As they waited, after a while, they called the taxi; and so, they found an outdoor pay telephone, nearby was a bus stop where they waited after calling the taxi.

First, they had to call the phone operator, who was very personable.

The operator asked, "Do you happen to be going to that David E. show?"

The driver, who liked a long show, was soon there and they all were singing songs with aloha?

Fanny commented, "Aloha songs, for me, I'm sure aloha songs are best.

"But to get there, we need a cab."

There was a hang up and a long, continuous buzz on the line.

Don Noh advised, "Let's call back."

And this time Don Noh was soon on the phone.

He announced, "If I can get there, I will sing as best I know how."

The operator replied, "Okay, play it again."

After a wait, the operator came back, and added, "Here is your cab connection." The phone was ringing and simultaneously the operator hung up.

Fanny was observant and said, "The cab is connecting. Here it is."

The cab pulled up and the driver leaned to open the door for them.

The cab driver said, "You guys singing an aloha?" Don Noh exclaimed, "I guess so. Maybe?"

The cab driver asked, "Do you know, that song is my favorite." "Yes, we sing it, and Fanny is dancing to a song,"

They were ready to do a song and Don Noh, who liked the song, jumped in; and had Fanny get in the cab. And that took them to the corner of the streets across town.

The cab passed by the statue of King Kamehameha on the way there, which was a ride between some one-way side streets, and then drove across a parking lot to the Queen Liliuokalani statue before driving head-on to the corner they wanted more toward Chinatown.

As they got to where David and Don Noh were possibly singing the song, the happily restless couple in the backseat of the very-plush cab, Don turned the door handle and they got ready to get out. The cab stopped and they were on their way.

Thereabouts, where David was set up; they were at a nice alcove, a grassy skirt about a coconut tree.

The songs he usually played so smoothly were with the guitar backing. Rather than mixing with the ukulele, a piano playing friend who had accompanied him once visited him on occasion, other systems of musical application allowed successful performance.

Still, they were another couple, who were a happily married couple, came through as the loyal friends they were.

And they had learned their friend the performer was going to come play at a new spot. As the other friends and patrons, who kept in touch as they played a daytime afternoon set, were at a friendly restaurant club and they came around for the albeit short performance, the clouds passed.

They came and enjoyed the music; they were often going somewhere to see who could understand the inspiration of the song. Then, Fanny's dance and that talent of hers were geared for the show.

She included music in his talents, he could sing and on occasion did an impromptu hula. They were talking.

He asked, "How long has it been since you've paid a visit to that performer friend of ours?"

She replied, "If it serves me right, it takes one hour to make the trip to see the performance; the site is open all afternoon."

He asked, "Now how long has it been since we've been to see the main attraction?"

She added, "With the tip that he is there and all, about fifty-one days."

It had been several months.

He continued, "That David! He sometimes plays guitar, he pays the guy to play the ukulele doing a show.

"Before it's over he may be switching to himself on the guitar. Now he is seeing the brighter side of programmed music; it has been seen at the main Talent Gallery for several months. And he shows up there."

It had been about five months though it seemed like years. It was like just yesterday since they had set out to see their friend. They were busybody folk, though they often set out to see some of their friends in some other part of the island and would be gone for days.

They had supported their performer friend David E., whom they regularly had acquaintance with. They were patrons of the professionals in that entertainment world, and would also be admired for record collections including Hawaiian music records. The performer's usual original music was hapa haole; and yet was accepted, appreciated, and collected by long standing performances.

Regularly performing, he included a small number of songs their other friends might have written. These were some outside songs, outside of their originally written songs, commercial jingles and the popular standards.

The fans were about to go on a visit.

He exclaimed, "I thought you'd be in a lively mood." He was looking at her, and continued. "And you're a hula girl."

She replied, "There is that."

David added, "Is there a friend who introduced you to me?" She replied, "Don?"

David clarified, "Honey! Howzit? Where have you been lately?"

Fanny added, "Do you want us to call you uncle?" He considered, "Uncle. It has a nice ring to it." "Yes! Uncle Don Noh!" Fanny chided.

Her uncle, who was a real traveler, would have allowed it.

There was a short moment that passed quietly as they were going to sing.

"I know people who have been to some of those places," Stan added.

A polite people, they were part Hawaiian.

David was in with being part Caucasian; and knew the racial melting pot, which was, none are the majority. He observed that Hawaiians were a lower percentage of the populations of, then, Filipinos, Caucasian, or Japanese as from newspaper reports.

Fanny had been hula dancing since early teen age. She had gotten together with a regular group, but then was separated for a few years a few years back, but had gotten back together at a new year's party and stayed together.

Often, they were barefoot and beaching. Don Noh had his ways.

He explained, "The rock is mainly observed in many waterfalls. Rocks are important."

He could go on and on about rocks.

After they got to where David was set up; and singing their regular songs, they enjoyed setting up their lawn chairs and listening to "Pretty Red Hibiscus"; then "Hanalei Moon," which was hula danced to.

Once David had recognized Fanny and Don Noh were in the audience. He might have paused. It was time for a break.

David welcomed them and looked them over and paused as Don Noh produced a couple of stones, these were musical instruments of native Hawaiian identity. Both rocks would be used as musical instruments (stone castanets). The stone castanets could keep a rhythm going.

Don Noh had used the rocks he had in producing an exotic sound with a coconut shell. The coconut shell was the half of a *puniu* and *ka* (knee drum and striker). David was with the adaptation, removing the sharkskin drum head and concentrating on the single hole opening, which had been for held with the open side of the coconut shell down on his jeans, he tapped it with the *'ili 'ili* (stone castanet), sometimes with just one stone and sometimes with the two stone castanets he was getting a syncopated tone; and by removing his finger from the hole he changed the tone a notch, raising and lowering the main shell opening on his pants, he created a muted variation; so there was offering a variety of note tones.

Don Noh liked it right away and said, "David, do try it out." David liked it too.

On their song "I See Fish" he did a rendition, and they liked it. In fact, the tones it could emit were within a seven-tone scale;

and with a knock-knock, sometimes syncopated, quality, many a tune could be had. And then, since Don Noh had collected four different coconut shells for the instrument: a rather small one, a really thick-shell smaller one, a really wide, thin-shelled one, and a normal one, there was a wide variety of percussion sounds that were made.

David commented, "It takes some time to get used to it, but you can play a tune, for sure."

Fanny and Don Noh had attended David's singing sessions at the lei stand, and had long hoped they'd get to where they were.

And there was an open mic at a nearby dining establishment that did like them.

Yes, they had come from their uptown flat and were now downtown, relaxing despite the numerous passers-by, and playing songs for those who were just taking care of their business downtown. They had exposed some of this talent, which was what was happening.

David, the performer, suggested, "Let's not fool around with these stone castanets or that coconut shell ringing out for a while?"

"OK.".

He went on, "Let's get those stones played in serious hula accompaniment as they were for many centuries, but as contemporary."

Someone in the audience was getting restless. He commented, "Well, play guitar and ukulele." David smiled and nodded in agreement.

He looked at a poster they had of themselves and thought, why don't we show stone castanets in the picture.

He commented, "Really, we don't know how to play castanets, much less these stone castanets!"

Fanny and Don Noh, who were out of the house and sometimes away traveling together uptown, would return. They had to answer their phone. They would also visit their performing friend.

They thought of their friend, who knew they were going to come. And in the meantime, David's friend, hula dancer and choreographer Lani was coming. She was going to dance for them again. This week was going by with regular performances.

David was outside near a street corner.

It was a while they played, Honey danced to a song, and garnered a welcome for the friends.

"I'd like to do "Hawaiian Sacred Spots "?" David suggested. 'That's a good one," replied Roselani.

"Would you like me to do "Lizard Man?""

And in time, they had many moments. They were mostly singing around Honolulu town and Waikiki.

Three

As he played, Fanny was warmed up and she danced the hula. While Don Noh and Fanny had been coming to see their friend perform, there was a song where she could hula to it, as usual went well. And she did it solo.

But sometimes, other dancers would come and enjoy dancing to this favorite standard.

Honey, who had taken some gift lessons of a Filipino dance, and tai chi like dance, which was agreeable to do, dancing became more respected.

Don, as he had become known as, formerly, had a Samoan friend, who gave him a lesson. He was an acquaintance. David, who felt encouraged to look at it as the hula practiced the youthful dance, noting elders seemed to practice it in a soft way.

Then, a hula lesson in which the *umi* was practiced was revered.

David, whose line went back to the eighteen hundred, had relatives that did hula, and family went back several generations, had relatives that did hula. They were both gratified by learning some hula. That was, at home or giving public performances, usually outdoors.

When David had come home from singing in public, it was to their flat on the south side of town. The flat was an uptown apartment, a level place and next door to where Don and Fanny, two of the most devoted fans a songster could have, who were regulars, lived. There was often a record player going at Don Noh's and Fanny's; and some of several records were listened to. Don and Fanny, who enjoyed lounging on their pillow strewn, thin-carpeted floor, had many records, and there were a lot of songwriter singers who were doing somewhat what David E. we're doing.

Hula heroines were coming along, they seemed to be there.

David E., keeping a keen eye out for their friend, Lani, the hula dancer who included choreographing certain legends into dance, was sometimes formal.

It was, then, good, Lani and Fanny came and did a hula.

Fanny said, "Hula dancers need to dance together."

David thought it could be done. So, he went into singing. Lani and Fanny had skill in explaining with their lovely hula hands ringing in the air; as they had hands that told the stories, so there was a pretty interesting story.

David, going along playing what songs they could, the song they had just sung was with choreography and he had said a lot before playing it to the small crowd.

They were playing in front of a small crowd, mostly passers-by, who had tethered on their way to lunch. The lunch breaks in downtown Honolulu included for many office and municipal workers, going to or by a mall, so wide; such entertainment as David offered could be done.

He was a little more permissive than before when it came to presenting hula dance in public like that.

There was a hope of someone dancing, Lani, Fanny, or their other well-respected hula dancer, Honey, who they knew had come to dance, which was for a while as they had been performing their best.

Their set, with their native musical instruments, fine instruments that beckon and support the dancers; and it was pretty daring to apply to the popular songs. They leveled practice with the native musical instruments that included nose flute, stone castanets, and the hula gourds, which often had rattles and feathers. They were quick to replace the bamboo rattles, which were specifically for keeping time, with stone castanets.

Keeping the time, David sighed in relief, and kept good time.

Their little performance had an end to it. They were about packed up with their musical instruments and the hula dancers went home.

David vowed, "We will be coming back here at lunch hours for the next few weeks at least.

It was six months later when David, still appearing at that spot, was comfortable; in folding chairs to play some of their songs. One of the songs they played was accompanied well, it also went well with the hula dance song had many covers by the top names in popular music as well as by the standard Hawaiian performers, so someone who was currently performing, was taking in David's show: and somewhere giving a similar performance.

The possibility that, with their hula dancer friends, who would arrive possibly soon, they would bring a brightenment to the day. The blue, tropic skies above reminded David that Lani's dancing would make the entertainment bright, and they waited for her. As they did, several of their regular patrons came and got comfortable for the show, which was usually with their hula dancers.

David, having noticed the hula dancers were around, thought they could do some of their music-oriented songs. He was right.

He was between songs and talking.

He commented, "Fanny will be here later." Lani replied, "Sure."

Lani came and sat next to Don Noh on the mat and smiled.

David, who had been expecting hula dancers to come, was waiting. She would dance, they would applaud, and there would be additional playing of music. As they warmed up playing the introduction, she was there performing.

There were quick reviews of their favorite songs going through his mind. He knew, before they got into doing the next song, there would be a good surrounding song to be included. And there was an overwhelming abundance of songs they could do. He was there, and he, too, was noted for doing a dance.

He commented, "If you have been playing a choice song here and there, the music is most applicable to you. But it's a difficult, musical piece, the chords and key, I mean. Why did you write it! I thought I'd better write it while it was fresh in my mind. I am better."

Some of the song players who visited sat and listened to their songs. An appropriate song was and David cheerfully played it.

It was not a hula song, and David noted Don and Fanny were sitting comfortably, which gave them a good feeling to be doing the song they were doing. They were increasing the volume of the song as they played, hitting the strings a little harder and noting the friends smiling.

There were some travelers in the audience, who had come and sat there. As they had recently got to that song, David thought the visitors were a type of tourist. They were travelers, who had come to have a good time, a reunion with friends, and staunch fans. They listened to the performance.

The small group of friends, a coterie of tourists who were from the mainland, had been David's contacts on the mainland, when they had gone there for a little while two years before. Now they were right there and listening to their performance, sitting relaxed and happy, they had come from a luau. David paused in the middle of the introduction as greeting parties, finally having exchanged greetings and shaking hands, relaxed, sat back, and enjoyed the musical show.

The group was touring from the mainland, also friends, who were comfortable.

The show was about to go on, and David introduced their favorite dancer, Lani. The dancer, having shown up ten minutes before, was pairing up with Fanny, and were getting ready to dance. Sitting comfortably, he always liked to watch Fanny dance, and the other girl was ready to dance.

He had asked them to dance to the standard, and "Hanalei Moon" was the song Fanny was expected to dance to. She sat next to Don, gave his hand a really good squeeze, stood, and took a place to the side as the show was about to go on.

David, who was continuing on the chimes ending of the previous song was almost finished.

The song they had played that had chimes in it was extensive at its ending with the chimes going on and on.
If they appreciated chime music and fine guitar work, they would enjoy this song, especially its ending, as it faded out into the quietude. David looked around, nodded and signaled to Lani so she should come and dance.

They played music with the dancers, Fanny was right there in front of the other two, telling the hula story with the dance music.

As David finished the song, the dancing slowed down and the dancers bowed down.

There was a quiet moment, a moment of awe and dancer appreciation.

David offered "Thank you for that dance, anytime you want to dance, you just come; we'll play for you to dance.

"Really a good idea. Come and dance regularly, we could always use the company."

"OK. Bye, now," Fanny replied.

But Fanny was bowing out, saying goodbye, the song was finished. And then, Don, who also contributed by singing, each of the many dancers put a dollar bill in the palm frond woven basket, bowed and left.

Don took off his cap, a traveler's hat, and bowed down. "Thank you," he said. They were usually in a hurry, and this time they walked to a nearby StreetSide and hailed a cab, which picked them right up and sped them off to a diner. They would be back after a while, David had liked their presence and said so.

He commented, "That was just the right volume of dance, and he liked the soft ukulele and guitar.

"Yes, it was good we had a wide range of song moods. They said they liked the singing."

Another time, they came and Fanny danced to their song.

David commented, "I had hoped and thought you'd come and be in a lively dance mood, and now you have come."

They were together, talking to the side.

David added, "And if you were my girlfriend, I'd remember the time there was also a friend who introduced you to me."

Fanny asked, "My friend, Don?"

David corrected, "No. Lani."

Fanny replied, "Yes, yes. Of course."

After the dance she returned to sit beside Don Noh, who was attentive. It was quiet. No one said anything. They were cool.

The hula was more often included in shows; and as Lani was still there, she had often done hula like the beautiful women portrayed in the advertisement of a luau offered to many visitors, she was top notch. So, besides being able to do a beautiful hula, the hula dance included in the overview of familiar songs, but with the possibility she would sing, David was ready to accept her performing.

Having grown up among backyard luaus, graduation parties, and birthdays singing and doing hula; also, at Christmas parties, retirement parties, and holiday events, there were weekly get-togethers she was there.

At this one time she had asked David to come and accompany her hula, he was going to.

All this was with the personality of graciousness. She danced modern hula, modern adaptations of older dances that went way back in time, she was familiar with Hawaiiana, and was giving the more traditional dance to a left behind time. This was somewhat with the addition of native foliage in the dress, which had been a lot of the dress in its time, which was before the islands were discovered by the west, and cohabitation. The native Hawaiians had seemed to always welcome newcomers, and Hawaiian hospitality was a native Hawaiian and local folk (adopted) attitude. Parties had welcomed newcomers.

The hula, having come from the dances of the further past, which were going with the designations of *kahiko* (ancient) were *auwana* (modern). But, mostly it was somewhat standard. For the many sumptuous luaus, sometimes regular rather happy parties, there was the familiar hula to a duo of the aspiring local talent. At this second largest entertainment capital of the world, this local entertainment found itself at such parties that

had taken on a standardization, and these had a host of songs that were suitable.

Lani's key time came. She had learned hula from a friend who had also been a model. She danced for the friend and was a member of the friend's hula group for a while. They had developed and enjoyed performing, some publicly, sometimes with her small group at certain park site stages.

Lani, who was set to go into public singing, danced for an event of David's enjoyment in presenting the little show he did. And she was one of the most attractive of the hula dancers that were around.

David was glad, as usual, to see her dancing.

However popular at home, the songs in the islands other than what David was playing were recognized by others. Others were often the hula dancers.

Similarly, other friends were coming by cab.

Meanwhile, in another part of town, a couple of David's coteries were Don Noh and Fanny. Honey was a dancer, and she had her boyfriend.

The boyfriend, Don Noh, commented, "Thank you for letting us do this song. It has been a joy to perform it. It's one of our favorites. We usually do our favorites and rarely get tired of performing them. Such songs as we play are additional to our other songs, which help to make it a combination act, where types of songs we usually do and others are expected to perform a little bit."

David replied, "That's OK, I play to have people give swell thanks for telling them about the hula dancing, and I 've heard they've got a few really new songs. I do think you would hula performances to my favorites. So many hula dancers enjoy hula dancing

Honey added, "For me to hula is a great, groovy thing. You guys."

They had been getting cab rides, and this was not so different. The taxicab driver commented, "I do have some other fares waiting to be picked up. Perhaps some other time, I can park and come watch."

Honey replied, "OK. Thank you for the ride anyway. And have a good night, you ought to do well tonight, it's a holiday weekend; isn't it?"

On the way home by taxi, Honey asked, "If you can make it come to one of our shows!"

The driver replied, "" OK, sure I will. Well, have a nice night." Honey replied, "Thank you. We'll try."

As Honey arrived where David performed, he approached her.

Their most recent song played, which had been well-received by the lingering shoppers, was in the air and they were warming up to do another of their songs. The crowds were quickly changing. The song they had played brought applause. The song was lingering in the air as they warmed up to do another song. This one brought Lani, the hula lady friend of theirs. She was spotlighted being nearby in the audience, and she agreed to hula to the song, which she had choreographed. She was there to perform; and was lucky they were including and expecting her to join the others if they were there to hula. If all would go well there would be three hula dancers. Before the next song was over, there were entrances and exits.

David asked, "Lani, as long as you're here, could you show us a little of your hula choreography?"

"Why certainly," replied Lani. She got up and came toward where they were playing.

Honey, who was there, had agreed to include her hula dancing with Lani. They headed to the front where David was playing the intro rhythms. They had a little time before coming to prepare to do this dance, a hula hula song.

Honey came forward to hula and David was in the back of the performers, anxious to see if the hula dancing would work. As the song ended, Honey was excited.

In a few minutes Fanny and Don Noh were standing up; they were headed to catch a taxi that was not far off.

They had been there an hour and were sharing the hula dance songs that David was playing.

As Honey had come forward to hula, David was actually anxious to see the performers perform, she was with Lani dancing her choreography.

Too, Honey and her friend could hear the music as they approached the front of the audience. David was standing by as he strummed his little alto ukulele, which he usually kept for special effects.

Lani said "I am teaching this dance, Honey. And if you do it, it will advance you in hula art."

As well as preparing her for choreography, as Honey learned from the well prepared Lani, and as David progressed the music to the recognizable song, she hula danced.

The song that David played while they were dancing, it was also a cue for Fanny to join them. Though Fanny was with Don Noh, who had wanted to be with the dancers as a partner on the stage, she stood to do it just herself.

This was a pretty good scene, it went into the night-time, and David was headed to a large pub where other performers were lined up to do acquaintances at an open mic. Fanny and Don, also had come. They had been to a school for performing dance, were professionally inclined, respectful at that hula was taught, and they had occasionally been included in a performance, which were often three yours at a time. So, who had once gotten a lesson in a Filipino dance, and David was familiar with a dance. While David was singing the familiar standard, Don Noh did his hula dance. In his singing and dancing, which was done just before the performer's break for a while, the effort had him quite worked up.

In the meantime, Honey was there, they had been part of the small crowd, some had put coins and dollars into their basket, applauded as their singing was that good.

David and Honey came together at a mellow point in the songs and she hula-danced to the music.

Lani, watching, liked the way Honey did it. She had done the best they could, as the beat of the dance was continuous as the performers segued, she bowed out the standard hula way, somewhat traditional.

David commented, "You are a good hula girl, Honey."

He looked around and commented, "Lani, now relax and be cheerful when dancing to ours. And we'll let you try and choreograph some of our other songs.

David smiled a knowingly smile, knowing she knew if played the intro to their song, the chords reminded Lani of the standards she had heard, that with the standard instrumental interludes, the vamp, that Don Noh, and others in the audience of about ten, who stood back about five yards as the dancers were vigorous, pausing. For a few moments their dance was to wait somewhere else until they recognized the start of the first verse of the tune.

There was a long pause as David took his show to a moment of non-hula. It was with a them, song that was new. He had the songwriting of a personal and enjoyable visit to that mountain top. Thus, the whole song developed into a sound that was described; but not like a chant. He could have gone on and on in that.

David said, "The continuum of the song has been tightened up over their occasional playing and practicing at their pad." It worked really well.

The few hula dancers they were in touch with their tried to explain the imagery with their dance. Lani was proud of her dance choreography and expertise.

As David played once more, another time, when just Lani was there to do the hula, he sang exceptionally well. Typically, as his chordal lead into the songs were, he gave a tune; and as he gave a glance to Lani to the side to dance, she was right in front of him. Honey, who was a little taller and a little blonde, stood to do some dancing with Fanny, who had come with Don Noh while Lani and Fanny were getting lined up and all set for doing the hula'. The dancers were lined up and it was really cool. As Lani was leaving Don in the audience, came up and coolly joined in the dance. They had on their blue muumuus. In the audience, David was wearing Bermuda shorts. The dancer's contrasting colors were their tops, and Fanny, who had gotten in the lineup late, was startling to see, as she was ready for the dance, and with it ensuing made a good impression. It was a swift tune, an original tune.

The hale (Hawaiian- house) in one song he was singing referred to an inspiration of songs they wrote. These songs were becoming familiar with a word in common usage of the Hawiian words.

David asked, "Do you get your ideas from a book?"

His reply was self-expressive. He replied, "Yes, sometimes I look up things in a pigeon book."

He was thoughtful, he had read pigeon language books and that one was handy, colorful with well used words like hale, keiki (Hawaiian- child), ono (Hawaiian- delicious), and had picked up some of the phrases and words as he had grown up.

There were drawings they once had presented as they performed.

He commented, "You know a lot of the names of streets are in Hawaiian."

He, again, self-conversed. He added, "Could be they are meaning things more definite.

"Some of the street names are easy to understand."

He played the song and Honey was observed by someone in the crowd.

The person called out, "I love you, Honey."

She looked sharply for the person. Maybe it was an old friend. Then, it was probably a figure she saw wandering off into the pedestrian traffic.

Honey was mumbling, "Do a hula song." David asked her, "What did that person say?" She replied, "I do hula all the time."

Honey had done the hula and had recognized the person, who with a happy smile; she had reminisced of his hula experiences.

David asked, "Who was that?"

She added, "That was a hula teacher I knew."

David asked, "Are you doing hula lessons these days?" Honey replied, "Yes, definitely, I see this teacher."

David commented, "I've done a little hula. It's pretty good."

Honey added, "Yes, I see that he has drifted off into the crowd."

They paused and glared to the back of the small crowd. As they paused and David dusted their instruments, the person wandered off. Afterwards there were few.

Honey joined Fanny, who had been waiting and as such had the cab ride waiting.

The cab driver exclaimed, "I like entertainment."

This driver wanted to hear his favorite songs as they were pulling away to a club in another part of town; in the distance David was singing. The dancing, which had stopped, and stopped Honey's hula, was still ebbing when the music, and excitement of it continued. The driver was satisfied, and continued on.

He sounded out, "I like giving them a ride to see their performance with their friends. They would make good friends. Meanwhile as David was performing, the show was going on...

As they performed, there was a song he did for Fanny to hula dance to, a new song of David's composition.

He commented, "Sometimes when it is quiet, we may hear the chirping of the birds. Yes! And then there are lizard chirps. Sometimes, more so than other times. Oh, those house lizards?"

In the back of the small audience, the taxi driver commented.

He said, "I don't know."

The quiet moment allowed them to think. Then there was a distant lizard chirp.

Afterwards there was another moment of quiet where he looked around to see the urban birds, doves usually.

Meanwhile, David was presenting a song at their site where they had set up on lawn chairs. People were intently listening; even some passers-by.

This was a time when Don Noh and Fanny had come to the set; however, they were recognized and welcomed. It was in between songs and the performers were warming up to do a light-hearted song of David's he was experimenting with. The little performance went well with impromptu hula dancing, which David wholeheartedly approved of and enjoyed; and an audience was watching.

After the performance, Honey, the hula dancer, happened to come around.

Lani had gotten together with Honey. The song was still being listened to. Then, David had given them blessings. And since she was going to dance hula in a few moments, they listened. David was getting daring.

He publicly commented on the hula. He said, "If Lani can come dance when we do some hula song, she knows the dance, the hula song is good, they like it, we like it, they can dig it. We can later do a ballad or something. But it is so good to have the three, who hula danced, Lani, Fanny, and Honey, to hula dance together

"Yes, it would be good!"

The hula dance, having become a familiar icon-like in the islands, was similar to the hula dance in the far past. One of many of the island groups in the Pacific, Oahu has its share of hula dancers.

It had been a few years since David, the songwriter-singer musician, found things hadn't changed much. Then, he sang and invited others to participate, usually hula dancers, and

occasionally with a karaoke machine, they were at it. They, at times, tried to sing like it was yesterday

There was a nice little group listening to them one day. It was early afternoon and there were many attendees. The day was wearing on and he considered the next song to sing. Fanny and Don Noh had come and were sitting, resting together. She had come to the place where he was already, and she was out of breath from a little walk.

She asked, "How are you doing, Uncle?"

Don Noh replied, "As usual, thankful for a visit. Now, I'm looking forward to a visit from Fanny."

She responded, "Good, and we'll ask them to do a song." He sighed in relief.

He replied, "You going to dance?" "Sure."

She had come late in the performance, it was their last set, and she was ready to dance if they played, and she had been, right away, enthused about dancing. So, as she got in front of David, who was aware she was just ready to get going into one of the songs they could play the coconut hula that she could hula to, she danced. The hula was good as they played,

David had thought good Fanny had shown up, and now Don Noh and Fanny are side by side, together in the audience. They were glad to be together, and they had fresh plumeria leis about on their shoulders. The plumeria, which was very fragrant and extended good feelings thereby, was fresh. These were regular attendees of David's singing, and they had also sung along with some of the outside songs they sang.

At a break, David handed his guitar to Don Noh, who could play it. He handed his ukulele to Fanny, who could play it, and

she would play and sing on the side, swaying to the dance as Lani, and their other hula girlfriend, Honey, danced to the song.

David had stood to the side as Honey and Lani got in front, Fanny shared the microphone with David, and they sang a medley of songs, which they went through fairly quickly. The audience was an appreciative group, they had been listening for an hour and put additional coins into the basket in front. David plucked out his favorite holiday songs, instrumental style, and Fanny played the rhythm as an audience looked on.

In a moment, they were through with the set. Fanny returned to her seat beside Don Noh.

Fanny said, "Thank you for holding my chair, Uncle." Don Noh looked at her for a long time.

He commented, "Thank you for the feeling."

Once, the season time came there with what was success.

It had been a good New Year and he commented, "Happy New Year."

This was early winter and music was booming from numerous stores and eateries. It warmed them, all playing songs. David was redoing one of his recently composed songs. His songs were not different from many other performers.

They were timely and regularly played their standards, including the local flavor of song.

They relaxed as carolers came by singing the familiar tunes. As the carolers finished, a bystander called out, "Do "Silent

Night",

"I know that, "replied the leader of the group. The carolers, who were accompanied by ukulele and guitar players, knew the song and gave their singing whole heartedly.

As they finished singing, the bystander asked for another song.

As some of the memories of someone of a tour group enjoying the show's regular performers described it, "They are pretty good," they were pretty good!

Those performers, who lived-on working in it and had been, however, expecting that show and its existence would be outstanding and most memorable, were comfortable; it was especially in that it was a lifestyle that they enjoyed, and saw. It was portrayed as comfortable.

As the one musician performer, who had been getting on in age, put it, "It was so good; we could get to this retirement age!"

Then, she had forestalled development of being in the forthcoming shows. Then, the retirement was a reward. Most such workers of this show were at retirement age and were working-on without that being noticeable. A doctor's approval was in place at times for some.

And so, one person's retirement, which had left the better part of this show languishing, was allowing him some rest. It was attentive people enabling him to remember a lot of his efforts.

And although some of the performers had retired, one performer had left some music to his business associates for their times of keeping up with him; because David, who was the best by now; and they were with a load of this most-liked, accomplished, and practiced general

The caroller's leader smiled, and sang the song.

David exclaimed, "The originators of that song would be proud of you."

"You're welcome," the person who requested, a nice man, replied.

The bystander asked, "Do you know?" Then the carolers sang.

The caroller's leader bowed and said, "Thank you. This is about time and doing songs is at this time of year. Thank you. We are going on."

It was a warmer set after this time. Seasons continue.

David was staying there, there had been others stopping by to listen.

He asked, "Okay, let's do it?"

After a moment they sang it out, and it being a nicely up-tempo song, it caught the attention of a number of passers-by. Those, who might like to find it in one of them for-sale CDs on the table beside the performers, purchased.

Honey was there, and she was attending the table. He smiled at the customer.

They had played through another season, their original song blended in with a standard here, and another song a friend of his had written was played, and he had asked that they include it in their music. The song was among the many songs they were playing this season. It was soon a new year and there were numerous celebrating parties stopping by them as they played. New Year's Eve came and went; and in the mid-January hustle and bustle, the weather was so nice, there were passersby who put numerous increments of dollar bills into their basket out in front of them.

As the new year was getting on, they were requested to play their song, which was a little educational, a little humorous, a little musical, and relaxing.

David, who was into being hip to the Hawaiian language had gone into working up his little song to a sort of thing that included the pigeon that was so around them then.

He declared, "In Hawaiian, 'E is a Word'."

"So, um, David, "Someone entreated, "we've been lucky to hear somebody say that they liked it. What they said was, "You know, with the 'eh' there, it's sort of a participle of a type, but it depends how you use it?"

David replied, "Yes, actually that's sort of two participles as one. It is so beautiful in language, because it can be used in more than one way."

Fanny, who had come, was listening.

Fanny added, "It has to be around you know." This was just around the corner from an eatery.

David asked, "What do you have to do with being called Uncle Don Noh?"

Don Noh replied, "Don, Ok.?" "I don't know?"

David was glad when Don Noh and Fanny sat on the beach chairs set up nearby; they relaxed and watched the man play their next song. The song had a rhythm that was like that of the sea.

Three

A long time had gone by when the song resounded, it was heard for some time, the ad libbing on it was what they envisioned as skin diving, and was liked, especially in its simplicity, it brought thoughtful reverie and smiles.

After the song there was a pause.

Don Noh asked, "Do you know a good fishing chant?" David replied, "No! But I have heard of a sea-chanty." Don Noh added, "I hope it's a good one."

David added, "I'm just in the mood for this."

Don Noh gave someone, also listening, a passer-by who was Hawaiian native and liked the stone castanets, the *ili 'il* (Hawaiian- stone castanets) *i*.

The person thanked, "Thank you for these. I have been looking for the right stones for a long time."

Don Noh commented, "It was a gift and I had rarely played them."

The person David gave them to was grateful but quickly left, walking away down the sidewalk.

"Let's play it again," David soliloquy-suggested. "You know," Don Noh replied, "that's not a bad idea."

"A song is a good song, but a good song is not the same as a chant."

David had parked near the performing site, and was out there playing the familiar standard, "I'll Remember You" (Kui Lee).

"You know, that's not a bad song," commented Don Noh.

David agreed, nodded affirmatively.

They were a long way from the lei stand benches, but they were doing good. Close friends were stopping by, and there were others performing in separate alcoves along the way.

Don Noh and Fanny were parked in a municipal parking lot near the performing site of their friends, David and were talking.

"You all might like this," David said.

He looked at Don Noh, who had a question in mind. Don asked, "Are you doing it now?"

David replied, "That's right. It's been announced that we're playing an island touring song.

Lani came, and she was soon over to see Fanny.

She confided, "Honey! Fanny is such a popular dancer! They'll sing for the touring people's tour. You know how Lani comes and dances with the songs."

"And she acts up!"

Fanny suggested, "I guess it's the song they wrote for her?"

Lani continued, "Well, let's listen to it and see if I can choreograph to it."

Fanny added, "If they do it in their next set, we'll listen to it, if they do it in their finale, we'll know it's going pretty good lately."

They presented it somewhat before the ending, which was a little more serious.

David was smiling as he commented, "We are playing this song with the instrument accompaniment introduction, and it plays well." They were well into the bridge, which had a usual good sound vamp, as it was supposed to be liked; and it was with a solo item that he played well.

He played it and went to the song that signaled the ending while Fanny and Lani were listening for their cue to come up and perform.

Lani professed, "Now that David is there, he's getting more vamp into the song, so we can hula to it more than usual."

Fanny replied, "I guess so. Show me."

Lani professed and practiced well enough to hula for her; and she did.

David was in a friendly musical organization of sponsored musical celebration, that was usually, when the hula girls came up to dance, it was often at a concert that had started out with just them; and it blossomed into a lot of friends and

musicians who were performing popular songs. The hula girls were planning on performing with David, when they got the cue, which was when their songs were in a jovial, joyful way. As most of the musicians, who were planning on coming on the stage with them there as they performed their well-known and well-versed exit songs, were members of a large, professional orchestra, they were welcome.

As usual, the ending was based on a simple exit song that blossomed into lots of people, hula dancers, and sometimes included other guests. Those who were part-time street musicians had the talent and just needed to get seen from time to time. While there were others, who were used to playing at an alcove of the street as David was, these were less well-known and enjoyed their acceptance by the observers of the public, as well as the professional bands, that informed the public through local newspapers. The lead singer of this whole conglomeration was David, one who was leaning toward becoming a professional, with his group David's Coterie, they were working well, and were singing their songs, including a fairly short, energetic, fun to sing, straight forward song that he had written. Others were based on some or one of his poems.

He was there enjoying the corner, like a concert of which included some of their hula dancer friends, as they did their own tunes.

After they sang, which had a room for ad libbing, their hula girlfriends, Lani and Fanny, were seated to the side and wanted to come up and dance. David was thinking about playing "Hanalei Moon".

The friends clapped loudly as they smartly blended their song into its ending, which went on amidst the applause,

hearty bow out of the song they were playing predominating and somewhat fading out.

Sometimes, David had come to the performance planning to play his lap steel guitar, a relic refurbished by a banjo player, in the few songs he was ready to do it with. As the performance was in front of other street performers, some were not necessarily musically oriented and were along the break dancing, juggling, and tap-dancing line, there were those from an energy to the street open mic, which had its own brand of folk tune performers. While there were some of them, who had thought they could join the performance, they did the regular songs which were actually getting harder to find.

David was expecting Fanny, at least, to come and dance too, and like many of their songs like that, and they did. Another song of their times, some of the songs. These were songs they had learned from earlier friends, some of these were well accepted as good songs to do.

David dug into a lot of info to find songs, some of his were of freewheeling ways, one was apparently of his acquaintances and was building up to standard level as by being in numerous shows, most of which were by friend performers on down the street, which has a way to have an acceptance of the song that was so familiar to the many listeners, which was a means to achieve a long ago, supposed, territorial style; which he had seemed to have agreements on, it was a very down pat style.

He liked the fragrant flower songs he had developed in the years previous, and they had a trusting basis for finding the right fragrances to impart in their song.

Eventually, his musical efforts were applauded, though by some people they didn't know, and their playing their own song time, and songs doing better. The old-time standard songs were worth making the effort, and they were appreciated. Nonetheless, they were into freewheeling ways, and those panhandling were often about. David was respected in getting their songs through to a live audience, and even more so, they were charitable. He found they were no different from most other songsters, albeit entrepreneurial based ones, of this time.

<h1 style="text-align:center">Four</h1>

As it was, sometimes Lani dropped by and gave them leis.

It was a typical day, and she greeted them with a lei strand from a lei stand. The traditional placing the lei around the recipient's neck and kissing them on the left cheek had meanings, and David was one to appreciate the meaning connected as was the flower behind the ear message.

A flower placed behind the left ear meant the person bearing the flower was, since this is the side that is closer to the heart, romantically taken. And the flower behind the right ear, they were freer from the romantic whole. The distinction grew and they got to be noticed by their audience as they regularly had the more serious right side bearing the flower given them by Lani, who seemed to give the significance more so to those.

David commented, "I'm seriously purported to be reporting a flower lei reception to have occurred."

Times went by with their playing music, not particularly tied to seeming ears of flower bearing, and the time passed to a present where they included a song.

David E., the local songster, had acquaintances of hula dancers, as well as others who happened by, at their makeshift musical island in the stream-like area near a corner. He commented, "Aloha."

Someone in the audience added, "Aloha."

There were a few regular attendees that day gathered to enjoy the song. Aloha was the word in the air, it was a reward. There is a lot of meaning into the word Aloha, and brewing a word with more meanings than most often applied, fits well for them to impart in their aloha songs.

After a couple of weeks of daily playing at the corner in front of a large hall, where there was usually a commotion due to a regular meeting and sometimes a show, the David, sometimes, group was beginning to become a bonanza of an extravaganza beginning with a friend, who had showed up and blown a conch shell. The sound of this conch shell was fairly deep, and yet they kept it from being too heavy, and loud, not without a gentle side.

They all listened to these conch shell beginnings, which was before these songster's music went forward with an ocean and seaside ambience to their songs, sort of an introduction to a set, and this was to go on to their Aloha songs. Their next song was a prelude for the ambiance songs of the seaside meant aloha, and was preceded with a song and followed with an aloha song. It sounded so heavy it was included in their aloha repertoire, but was relatively a meaningful experience. the conch shells. There was a story and a song, and with regards to the conch shell.

David explained, "I used to go to the beach, and when the swell was hitting, before going surfing, there was a blowing of a conch shell like this one.

"Aloha, my friends,"

A welcomed taxi cab driver there taking a break near where they were about to play some of their songs.

"Aloha, "he replied.

On the other side of their little set up, a coffee wagon, which included tables and chairs, two tables and stools were rarely vacant, the coffee was poured out for passersby as well.

And the vendor called out, "Aloha". Soon, his customers were filling the area around and he was right about there.

David often found spare time in a prearranged set to play a song or two that they were experimenting with. They had regular refreshments from the coffee wagon nearby during a break, which was when they were about to be playing their aloha set, starting with going to an "Aloha Lady".

They noted, the coffee wagon appeared to be Auntie's, continuing her business, there were a few flowers there.

Where would all the aloha tubes lead?

They played with a heavy beat as it sounded like an anthem, and was well appreciated for linking the songs together. If some of their songs had a marching rhythm, and if some of them were up tempo, there would still be attentive, small traveling groups, to hover about nearby and respectfully watch, before going on their tour as it were, usually a rendezvous after shopping.

Once a small traveling group respectfully watched and waited for the end of the song to applaud. Then, he played on.

And they hummed it so pretty soon, they were fading out. He was soon introducing the song to the numerous people who were stopping by and going on. This was near a bench, and they had a little bit of lawn there to park themselves. The area near a park bench was where David played their music, where they practiced to groups, and noted, "There's some landscaping here."

A bush background was at this place and extended about ten feet high.

David's introduction was short, was a good song to set the periodic listeners to their performances.

David believed aloha would work its way as such and be useful for their opening songs, which were to a particular seaside set. This was while they were situated on the grassy area in the midst of one long, near downtown shopping and business mall, that one was where numerous people stopped to listen to them and donate to their upturned palm frond basket.

He was talking about it.

"I've been toying with this song for the last couple months, and now I'd like to sing it, and keep it in mind."

"Probably for the rest of your life," David said. David was together on it,

He commented, "I've been backing up hour songs for so long. And I've got to pick up the beat. I start with a few background chords, and you go on to your playing the choruses."

"Here goes," he added.

There were about fifteen seconds of rhythm by hitting his intro chord, holding his guitar chord and the guitar by the neck for a second, then tucking the guitar under his arm before strumming on.

David plucked a few notes on the ukulele, and then droned out. It had started out well and since it drew some shoppers and other passersby, who stopped, looked, and listened, they continued.

As they paused in their singing they stopped requesting audience participation, and thanked their lucky stars, it looked like Lani was going to demand their performance of a hula song. The time for this performance was coming nearer.

Then their presentation was becoming more serious and in some cases over humorous. That seriousness which was sometimes expected found them trying again a new song. And they played one after another of their new songs, some of their songs would be piled on top of a fairly high pile of song sheets; and for donation, passers-by could buy one for a dollar.

David had this worked out, and had a satchel with extras to possibly sell.

He well knew, among the stock entertainment field, also had the interest of workers in the area, who paused at their show area, usually around lunchtime.

But most of the other showmen needed a special show-place and they were looking for a high or low place right by a lot of people walking by. They wanted someplace that they could sing.

Some few miles away there was as it was at some times during the year, a carnival. The stage there they had the opportunity to play at was next to a side game.

Then, David, who rattled off song titles to a few pass-ersby about the side game next to them, where throwing and knocking a thing off a shelf was rewarded with a soft, stuffed animal, which was a background for them. As they sang their

a popular, old time version, while in the booth show-men were offering the stuffed animal for their throwing tal-ent, it went well.

They sang a song made popular on this theme, and they sang their songs as their attempts to present them were, often, while a coconut was being thrown to knock a thing off a shelf. On the side the postal coconuts were sold.

These were the case and as the songs and rewards were going on, the small change flew often to their upturned coin basket. They had accumulated enough in that, that it was beautiful.

Six

David thought, if they played in a park later, and this was where the parade ended, there was a carnival, and it was entertaining. As they had entertained many individuals who had enjoyed a coconut toss next to a nearby song, and dropped their coins in for them, these other people of the show enjoyed sometimes playing their songs.

Sometimes, playing at a beach park, where there was carnival set ups, they played near them, the beach carnivals were usually practical sessions. These showplaces often signaled a fair was coming. Playing at a fair, which included some show people, developed. After the occasional such show, their regular outing of regular performing served to increase their regular enjoyment of their songs, and they took off their hats.

David, who enjoyed being there, was talented, and sometimes David showed as a good guitar player. His catalog of old folk songs was interesting, and an occasional novelty song helped when they did play at that fair next to an arcade. Their lovely songs fell into the area of island ambiance regularly, and if it was not for their poetry, they had the talent of composing songs of it, some of their fans would have just been satisfied with David's sometimes playing a twelve-string guitar that he rarely used or brought out.

Sometime ago, they had played away from the many ways and places they were playing, playing to those who were visiting the lei stand and hiking forest trails. Now they were near a large park, or a wide boulevard, a mall, or beach park. Their songs that had once been heard by a couple of lei vendors and a host of tourists, where they wandered around as they were listening to their singing they listened.

It was such a good time, for someone who was well into singing, was someone moving songs such as their own. That aloha in a performance was with a performance. Then, sooner or later, a hula dancer friend would show up and they were soon juggling their repertoire. To suit the hula dancers was a song to test the possibility of singing the song.

As a song faded out, and yet it inspired they're further playing, they played on. After finishing playing their signature opening of aloha songs, they were noticed by some other performers looking for songs to include in their act, those who did were rewarded because the songs they offered usually fit the bill.

He hit one more chord and held it, Sam was daydreaming momentarily expanding on their songs and their acceptance into the performers, as the public passing by looked on and around. David, often looking for a song buyer, had recently met one who would be about five minutes before they could get into paying for their next song's publicity. David was nonetheless daydreaming.

The next time they were playing came, and they were doing their standard song introduction set at the usual location, which was near a series of grassy areas set in the cement. There were rain showers this time, that like so many such times, had led them to head home. There were the surprise blessings of rain showers and nobody minded.

David, who were long time high school local grads, had a quick pack up and exit plan for when shower weather occurred. This time they would go to a nearby park gazebo, which remained an empty gazebo　　even after he left; in an hour or two, he'd be where they waited for the shower to stop. It wasn't long before they could go back to where they had been playing not far away. They started with their next song, which was an original, though they had a series of folk songs to include.

As the seriousness was supposed over, and to the listeners, some who were just passing NBA, witnessed their performance over the shoulders of the small crowd of sho enjoyed the performances of David's, some had come out of businesses in the area, time was sort of passing by as being in the considered meaning of their songs.

There was song of birds, and there were songs that were folksy and alluded to the pineapple picking time they both had had once, enjoying the passage of time there.

Seven

As David had been into that and was sometimes around, considering the meanings of their songs. There was joy in the aspects of a goal being achieved. And with those who considered among other things, this somewhat temporal happiness, they would find peace, and in the absorbed peace of the songs and music they had developed, they went on and sang their similar songs they had listened to. And many a radio station regularly performed ways to their peace of mind, through the occasional stock song.

David was thrilled every time he performed their song. He found it interesting as he pounded down the strumming with an extra heavy bass beat accent.

Few comical songs were at first sung, then, they came up with the aspect of encroaching on the more jovial side of such things as the language flurry, And many walked to nearby them as they finished the introduction.

The effect of playing these songs was so good. He wondered if he shouldn't try and make it more accessible, since they usually kept the volume at a legal low. With volume, the lyrics were that good, it remained appreciated.

David explained, "As I am in between songs, now we're sitting in front of our set, there are people in front, listeners who know us and expect a dramatic tale to take place."

"There is that," He replied.

He was thinking of their one ballad.

There was irreversible happiness, and they partially considered the mentality of this song with regard to the ambiance, which was seaside.

David was singing and was gliding the musical accompaniment, improvising at the end of the song. This was a time when they played standards that had gotten some mainland familiarity. Songs like these were played by folks in their homes for parties. They played the current day standards.

His hula friend, Honey, asked, "So, where have you been skin diving?"

David replied, "Beyond the reef, but not recently, but I remember vividly, lots of fish; so, I will tell you exactly how it is."

He added, "That's right; if we're in the middle of the sea."

There was a time in their musical accompanying and improvising to the ends of the song that they let the music take them on for quite a while, perhaps allowing some improvisation. Songs like these were what they played.

He hit his bar C chord on the eighth fret and held it, its resounding increase as he held up his guitar by the neck, a little bit away from his body.

The song was slowly fading out, finally finished, and that last resounding chord David had hit was thoroughly enjoyed by the people sitting nearby in lawn chairs. They had brought refreshments and were enjoying themselves, and some folks were sitting on padded mats on the small well-kept lawn portion of the area around some coconut trees that had, actually, been planted there mature when the landscaping for that part of the sidewalk had occurred.

David, working up their performance quite a bit from the times they had lingered on park benches. Listening for applause, there were some fourteen people in front of them that applauded.

David commented, "Right. on!" Then, he complimented, "On."

But their joking was through. Then, his music was going on with a song,

David suggested, "Let me do a good job on this last song I wrote, and "I See Fish?" is turning out best."

He agreed, "Okay."

As they went into the introduction of the song that Frank had recently written, usually he wrote with a long instrumental introduction, there was this particularly cute introduction that they had added, and he was doing it solo.

He was hopping from one chord to the next, strumming.

David commented, "You all might like this. There is some fishing element, kind of here.

"We were once playing for a group that included those who liked to fish. They were talking, and one of the fishermen reminisced that he had hooked a humuhumunuku-nukuapua'a. The fishermen who had been under a supervisor had helped it out and taken the fish off the hook and tossed it back into the water where it swam off. Quickly, the fisherman recast his line.

He commented to another of the fishermen, "I thank the supervisor for taking the fish off the hook, partner. That is right-on. Now, there will be more fish to catch."

The supervisor added, "By letting that one goes back, it was struggling to get off the hook, there will be more fish to catch."

The partner added, "I keep a steady footing on the slippery rocks there at that spot where you are, were, standing."

David added, "That is a good one. There are lobsters out there."

David added, "In season." He smiled, then said, "The birds were flying by."

They commented, "There was a turtle sighted. And as the day progressed toward sunset, every one of the small groups of shorelines fishermen went home with a few fish. They had gotten a little salty from the spray, and it seemed the beach was dry and sandy and the fine grains blowing in the wind for hours there had embedded them in it, they had gotten it into their hair and skin. They brushed the sand off, but still there remained some.

"Then, they were getting tired from standing and casting their fishing lines, some of their lines were just tied on to the end of the long bamboo pole. So, they packed up to go home. Eventually, there had been waiting for everyone to get into the vehicle."

David had introduced the song that he was inspired to sing, and they added his instrumental accompaniment as they were singing. After the last sounds of the song completely faded out, there was that moment for comment.

David commented, "I have been to the beaches, not lately, and been diving. I saw small schools of manini (a type of reef fish) and I was looking to get some. I took a few Hawaiian sling (a type of spear gun) shots, holding my breath, and ducking down below the surface, missing each time."

Drawing the Hawaiian sling is actually a little awkward, but being lightweight allows it to be drawn and shot numerous times in one breath.

David continued, "Some kumu, a reef fish, were in my view but they are quicker, I missed; then there were some in small schools, a few that were bagged, and later steamed."

He had gotten used to hearing his Hawaiian sling spear gun bang and clang onto the reef and rocks, usually totally missing the fish.

Such fish were better caught. Their size and age, therefore, a concern, make them easier to spear, these fish are less likely to hide. And one is careful when eating them, they steam nicely, but they are known for having small bones, you can enjoy some. They are fairly common and the bones are plentiful.

David commented, "It is pretty nice swimming around the clean waters outside of the reef where it starts to get deeper, without the wave currents and surges of the reef."

There had been a time when he had been skin diving when he was visited by a honu (sea turtle). And there had been a few that were on the scene.

Another time he had noted an unusual sight, there was a nice *aku* (tuna) fish that jumped outside beyond the reef. It made an unusual sight, it was not so close to shore, but memorable. It was a large fish, and one didn't worry about the bones.

Someone, who had seen him playing by this Auntie lei stand, liked to listen to their songs.

He commented, "I had been working in the pineapple fields, picking in those days not too long ago, and me and my friends were going diving after work, which had been hoeing that day. We had been pulling suckers (shoots from the base of the plant) the day before, and putting them in the boom."

They replied, "I don't know! And I know one doesn't skin dive there anymore. But we thank you for reporting your experience."

David sang the word, the name of the state fish, in, which had been a challenge to express in the allotted time of the note; other variations of the name would be tried. He thought it was a well-practiced point. The conversation in the song was brief, and was most well-spoken, most assuredly enthusiastic.

He announced, "This is not the ' song you know.

"You know, this is the song that goes back before post discovery. You know, when the islands formed over millions of years from being volcanoes dried for millions of years just drifting in the sea ever so slowly."

They replied, "Yes, I know."

They paused, and he got the tempo going strumming skillfully, and started singing their one song that introduced a string of ocean-oriented tunes. Sam was right there with it. And then it would be on to the new tune. Together. David simultaneously enunciated. Then David added. This is it.

They waited for a moment and looked at each other pleased with the introduction.

David commented, "Okay, on with echo-like comments that took them into playing.

There was a sigh of relief that went up from the few visitors they had, some were standing, and those who were attending possibly would dance. This was a good sign. The sigh of relief relaxed, so they sang their comfortable music.

Perhaps, before very long, they too would feel the old trade winds.

"You know, David,' 'they commented, "I once went body surfing."

"Yes," David said.

"I found puka (*puka*- hole) shells in my trunk pockets." "Puka shells?"

His hula dancer girlfriend looked at him.

David added, "You could walk along a stretch of beach after a big swell, and I mean you still can, and especially, you might find a puka shell between your toes. The luck of having a puka shell be found right, exactly under your right foot, and if you find enough you can easily collect enough for someone to make a choker necklace."

"Or anklet?"

"Other times, if there is no big swell, maybe all you would find is the little shiny shells."

"And if it's the right place, some starfish dried hard."
"Among the puka shells."

A spectator, sitting up, most in front of them raised a hand and simultaneously commented, "That's kind of lucky. Finding

puka shells right between the toes? Most times you have to keep a sharp eye out for one, the day goes by and you get some."

David commented, "It could be beginner's luck." "Gotta be," replied the spectator.

"Gotta be," David added.

Someone was wearing nice rubber sandals that had a prong between the toes. He looked down for a moment and looked up and thought, 'there's a puka shell that could be found right there'. They commented, "You know, David I'm not really that crazy about wearing shoes on the sand, the beach and shoes don't usually go together. If I am in a hurry or something! Maybe one would? But nothing to do with the sand that would fill my shoes. If it was really soft sand!"

"But I would be glad to go hiking with hiking shoes around HanaUma Bay. It would be really good."

"Yes, you would need shoes, that lava rock up there about the crater is fairly abrasive to say the least. It's sticky and gets hot. And on a hot sunny day, it's extra hot."

David noticed their patron, the spectator who was there, was wearing a puka shell necklace.

The spectator explained, "I picked up all of these puka shells from a country beach after a big swell. I strung them all up over a few days in the following afternoons, and finally tied the string when it was the right length. There was still enough room for someone to get it on."

"I have one, too," David commented.

David added, "Me too." He scooped from his bag, inside, and waved the healthy puka shell necklace around in front of the spectator.

The spectator commented, "I like that one."

Their day was going to another day. They came and played again.

Six months later, David was still coming to play at that spot.

Some of their songs changed.

The friend announced, ""This is the one of the songs that adds us off on a musical journey. And they played them both.

David added, there are those very long-ago times we think of in the islands. In that past, the islanders have allowed some speculation on their civilization."

David's friend added, "As current residents in more recent times, we look to the area of Waikiki in front of a queen's estate."

"Queen's Surf?"

Daviid added, "Yes, there is a Queen's Surf surf spot."

David;s friend commented, "And now, you know what, there is a song that David wrote."

Sam added, "It's one of the nicest surf spots there is." "Queen's Surf."

"So, we try to present the song we have written for that spot, which is part of a greater surf spot, which includes the outsides of the Waikiki surfing area!" speculated David.

"Outside, it's First Break."

"Queen's Surf's farther out? I don't know?"

They played their song, which was followed in suit with David, who had suggested part of it too, and found it exhaustive, though an accomplished song, one of numerous *hapa haole* songs that they took great pleasure in presenting, he was often a little exhausted after singing it.

The appreciation of a songwriter was, in a word or phrase, a tradition that went back years. It was a local tradition for the locals appreciate the songwriters with many gifts, usually of food.

"Then there are those traditional hundred years back songs and chants. Some people like to accomplish them," he explained.

David added, "It's like a lot of songs, they are kind-of like little time capsules."

"Little news clips."

When he had been young, he had surfed at Queen's Surf, the spot that held a surf meet for juniors, and he had a good time. In the wonderful surf there, the waves rolled in, easy to catch. He, too, had done some wave riding when younger.

David announced, "I got a picture postcard from a friend who had been visiting here, it was a picture of Queen's Surf in which the waves were gently rolling in with numerous riders on the wave happily watching out for the others on the wave, happily riding toward the shore, or where the waves were diminished and not supporting wave riding."

In some cases, there were times when the waters were very powerful, during a big swell, the outside breaks coming alive and sparking reports of such size in antiquity it was hard to believe. It would be very serious for a surfer to wipe out on such big days, even the period of such waves, even for the experienced wave-riders, would be a time of provocative wariness.

David was comfortable then, they played a warm song of the surf.

This was entertainment informal, which before long as they were singing this song using a set start, was of a set of wave riding and beach appreciations that could, perhaps, be attributive, as well as many other surfing sites.

The sight of surfing, which was a grand sight that many came many miles to the islands to see, would have been grand as they played. And some patrons imagined the sight, and wondered if he weren't visualizing as they sang, the wonder sights of surfing.

Some of the patrons were patrons of the local music altogether. Some of these people were David's friends, and were attracted to them for their singing and original songs. There were recognized performer's names and faces on posters outside of entrance ways to many a pub that had entertainment as well as coffee-houses, and the patrons paid visits from time to time to these, as well as contributing to the David's performance including, who were going on singing songs.

One of the songs that could be heard. David had some beach experiences, body surfing sometimes. There was a sweet hula dancer, Lani, who had been at the beach and liked them for their singing. She had waited for them to return up the beach to its parking area and gazebo. They had liked Lani and knew her as a hula dancer.

David asked, "Lani, we knew you as a great hula dancer, and wanted to meet you. Would you like these puka shells I just found?"

Lani perked her head up and stretched out her hand, where David dropped three very nicely formed, large puka shells he had just found when walking up the beach from the surf.

David was pleased too, to meet Lani, who was a fan.

After about half-hour, they had retrieved their musical instruments and were singing in the gazebo. Then, he sang.

David had a collection of shells, and some were being made into jewelry presentations. One was noted for having certain mussel shells. He paused and took out a container of kukui (a tree that produces a nut that produces oil suitable for suntanning and care of the skin) nut oil. He poured a little out and rubbed some on his arms. He offered it to Lani, and she took it.

"Thank you," Lani said.

She poured out and rubbed some on her arms and shoulders, nose and back.

"Can I help you?" He asked.

'Yes, I would like some on my back."

He poured some out and slathered it over her well-tanned back.

"Thank you," she added.

David was wearing a puka shell necklace he had just put on. It had one nicely fluted large shell at its centermost point that had been gilded.

Someone commented, "They've got a *pipipi* shell necklace at several stores."

David replied, "We know."

They added, "Yes, they are actually, really nice."

David added, "I usually like to do the "I See Fish" song.

While keeping to the beat of the song, he compressed the word and was naturally happy. He found other songs in his trying effort, and effort that was appreciable because it was important, he had to take more breath to say the entire song word, and breathing and skin diving went hand in hand. He was sitting up and listening, his basket was still catching, like a coin.

It was a normal daily gig. Time went by and they were getting better.

Three months later they included their catchy fish song, they had played it to a small audience, and were resting.

Nine

The surf was aside for the time being and David had relatives on the Big Island to visit. He had visited there and reminisced about living among the ferns and 'ohia trees in the uplands, too, and had gone to visit relatives on the Big Island.

But life goes on, and so he was living with memories that could be larger than life.

They were both familiar with the legends. The one of the 'ohia tree and the *lehua* flower bore out some views of the legendary volcano goddess. Pele, as the volcano was one thing. But Pele as a person, in the antiquity of times past, took on a favorable view as a historical person. The legendary volcano goddess was of the times with reference toward mortal man. When the volcano erupted, it was an angry thing. And when it came through with a lava flow quickly overriding a large tract of houses, or 'ohia trees, which was part of a familiar story and legend, the view was that volcanic action needed quick solutions.

As the legend of the 'ohia tree' followed with the *lehua* flower, the scarlet spindles welcoming bees, the story was understandable. The legend of the tree as the man, and the flower as the man's woman, were understandable. The jealousy of the volcano toward the tree and flower was compatible with normal human jealousies, such as a human-like volcano being jealous of the flower for the tree.

He enjoyed the lore and found that, since it was described in numerous books of legends of the islands going way back and becoming scientifically depicted; do not take it all for granted; do not take it as exactly well-put. In the reinforced literature, reinforced by supposed celebrated song and hula of the same subjects, the celebrations of hula took precedence.

When he came up with the song as a legend, it took a few years to check on the documentation of the legend. Indeed, there was such a backup.

David started out in doing the song, "Legend of Lehua" with a phrase, "If you pick the flower it will rain, it is the tears of Lehua for her lover, 'Ohia."

They sang the song once with gusto. Though usually they remained restrained as the rather sensitive subject, which was appreciable given living in a land where freedom of religion was guaranteed by the national constitution, they included it.

He reiterated, "A legend of the *'ohia* tree is: if you pick the flower it will rain the tears of Lehua, which are for her lover 'Ohia."

He commented, you know, I came to believe in that legend when I was younger. Even then I knew it was just a legend, but I guess you need something to believe in when you are young. And that legend seems to be it. Especially when you have read the complete legend of the ohia tree and read the story in several books of legends; plus heard it described by respected old-timers.

"Believe what you want. But it's a popular, well-read legend if you ask me. That legend is in numerous books. There are some aspects of that legend that may be represented, and in hula fest."

There was a time of thought that was appreciable. He added, "Ya, I know there's that hula fest.

"I think that legend goes beyond reality and so the belief is maybe able to convey there is an importance of events like volcanic eruptions, which in this case has them of the past.

"Like the lava flow destroying a treasured ohia grove story. "I guess there is that one."

David sat quiet for a moment and it was respected. They were deciding to do this next song, somewhat of a Pele song.

He plucked a string at random, it resonated fading out. Sometimes they did this serious, heavy song portraying the event of the Pele, goddess, and the lehua tree. They had heard about the volcano in the news, it was not an unfamiliar, nor unexpected event for the local people of the island of the Big Island, especially since it was just one more in a string of eruptions. So, the more the people who moved away in fear of the inevitable lava flow, they note that the lava had eventually claimed this or that landmark, whether it was a treasurable grove of 'Ohia trees, or a miraculous and beloved tide pool, which was warmed from the heat of the lava underneath for hundreds of years, this was numerous groups of friends had occasion to enjoy the bath by the sea. There had been one such time for many visitors to that part of the island, just near the shore, a surf sport there allowing mellow wave riding.

The lava flows happen from time to time and it was evident as David had been about there when younger. That certainty, that the volcano was extinct and ceased its hundreds and thousands of years of flows would be depositing his trust in age, and the land from it, which had over many years produced numerous fern forests and areas where 'Ohia trees grew. The lava flows, which had frozen in that moment of flow had stopped hard, where lava shelves that could seem to have times before, he envisioned as typical rolling swells at sea.

Then, there was no one, nor the islands: way out at sea.

They sang their original songs in memorial to the place and legend that had so covered it with a lava flow. The song, which was like a super mini novel, but then it had a warm experience being that it portrayed the shore pool, was somewhat lamenting.

David was often presenting their outer island inspired songs. Sometimes they did it with a parody borrowed from folk songs. that derived from a romantic song. This was one that had bypassed the numerous parodies and simply stretched out the moment of song. Then, he did their song, which was sounding tuneful, and was as an original song verse.

And he noticed Don Noh; and he was a little late.

Don Noh and Fanny, who were pretty hip to legends, did come back to enjoy David. They stayed somewhat out of sight, sort of impossible to do in a group in front of the duo, but to the side and in the back of a small crowd they enjoyed the music they heard, not disturbing their friends while in the middle of performing.

David noticed they had come.

He suggested, 'As long as we're doing songs of that volcano legend, why don't we do this song?'

"Sure!"

In a moment they were strumming with their instruments. They played a regular bottom note and sang verse one and two of their song, and were with one verse, off to a beautiful vision of high-altitude lava production i.e., the top of a mountain, the tallest in the world, from the sea floor that is.

There was a usual, small crowd there one interesting day that included band leaders and members of a group who were on vacation.

They were happy to hear someone performing a country & western tune on harmonica. What interested others who had come to hear was really more of a folk song. David would have played longer, but having preferred it without spoken interludes decided not. There were those there who recognized it and applauded for a long time after the song. After some of the band members applauded, they drifted off to shop.

The applause continued, with songs, and as Don Noh and Fanny were standing up, they left David in the distance strumming and singing.

After the song had subsided, he hit a few chords.

People that had gathered to listen were often restless shoppers, and visitors.

Further away, Honey, who was becoming a normal person to visit them, came to see them. David undoubtedly would welcome her since she came, she immediately agreed to hula. She had come and Don Noh and Fanny were still there.

Perhaps there would be hula to include in their presentation.

Ten

David commented, "This song has us somewhat vacant with regard to memories of seeing the birds, the o'o are so rarely seen, as well, the koa'e. Even if we had hiked the remote trails of some islands, we probably wouldn't see or hear them.

"A curious 'iwa bird may fly closer to the shoreline folks sometimes. When one is at the beach, someday, you might look up and these birds are quite large."

David looked at him in wonder. There was a momentary pause of the small audience there, who were just as still and enjoying the talk, just sitting there listening. This was the place for a city bird to drop by.

Nearby the performers to the side, there was a vacant bench near them, a dove dropped by and perched on it, like to listen to the singing. He added, "I still find it hard to believe there are native Hawaiian birds flying through the evening."

Lani came then, and commented, "The Pueo."

David said, "They fly through the twilight, maybe just a dark shadow flying to a perch."

Lani commented, "I have seen a few Nene (Hawaiian geese) by a pond. Yes, the Hawaiian goose is supposed to be around swamps and ponds."

David commented, "You know, I do believe I have gotten used to thinking of a sandpiper, it seems there are a few of these birds here-abouts. That is a researchable bird. And the nene (Hawaiian goose) is seen, it was kinda a long time ago, and researched in a library. I saw a Nene (Hawaiian goose) in a book."

"Yes, you can go and check out a book, and research while you're there, returning books is important."

A small block of myna birds had settled on the little bit of lawn that hosted a lamppost opposite their spot on the sidewalk where they were set up, and the birds were chattering and prancing about as they did. This was near a bus stop, and a small group of three chickens came strutting nearby. There was one rooster, they were feeding on the grass nuts and seeds as well and the rooster started toward our performance set up, then one of the hens quickly, as they do, cut him off and seemed to direct him to the grass, where he did some pecking.

David waved at the rooster directly causing it to go in the opposite direction. A hen jumped back.

"It's okay," commented David.

The chickens, which were red, had probably been brought to the islands by canoe hundreds of years ago; they were quite colorful and were around again and Sam waved at them again.

They scurried away. He continued to wave his hand at them as they moved away further.

There were a few people there watching, and listening to their song, they clapped as a rare sight there, a cattle egret bird circled about, ever so gracefully and landed. There were some small gray doves, and a host of larger white doves flying about over time at this, and other similar places set up for one to play music.

The time passed while performing a song! And afterwards, he returned the instruments, a guitar and ukulele, to the cases.

They did fairly well this day with a few extra five dollar bills, a little more than usual, from their small coconut frond basket that they had used for a long time; since performing in recent years including at the old lei stand fantasy park. There were some good donations.

There was a good long while with the song's fading out, the chimes he played were long dead. There was applause which seemed to linger in the air after the song was finished.

He said, "Yes, the lifestyle of the birds is there. "There are a lot of birds flitting, flying, and prancing about."

"Myna birds can be humble, seeming human.

"Myna birds can be cool, Myna birds can be chic and appreciable, they can do what they do.

"They do know how to carry on; and chatter. away"

David had quickly changed the string on his guitar; the lightest 'E' string had finally given out!

He packed away his alto ukulele in a bag and remembered, both ukulele and guitar were to be included in the performance.

He had sat across the street for a while on a municipal park bench, waiting to start earlier, thinking of those birds. There were some that had become endangered species, they might have once been in the exact spot where he was sitting.

He thought; replacing a ukulele string was not to be taken lightly; tuning his guitar and humming a few verses of one of the songs he had written would do wonders; together the instruments were valued. In that he usually did this, though it had been written about as a little out of current style, there were some advantages.

Then, a few people watching, paused as the singer-songwriter was amusing.

David spoke, and then started singing. The silence was broken and the attention on them prodded them to play louder. Some of the chords of the song remained as the end resounded. He had been playing the song of naming birds in with new chords being played.

He commented, "We got our bird's names here checked out, some are with official titles like endangered species. The song was supposed to consider threatened and extinct birds, so it may sound a little mournful, for the birds are not to be found."

There were whistles and calls found in some birds that he imagined, and adding to the song as he sang worked. Usually! He listened in his free time to recorded whistles and bird calls. These, usually from hard-to-get-to rural areas, were appreciated and listened to.

He explained, "In our home, in the evening, we listen to recorded whistles from rural areas. I can hear one over and over in his part of the house. We carry these sounds with us for one moment in our performances, as part of one song that may be implemented with an authentic sounding bird call.

"Sometimes it is a little quaint when the quiet we hear is accompanied by the chirping of, not the birds, but the house lizard.

"Some of the birds are very little. It is surprising. They can be heard." There was a pause, and he added, "On record."

There was a moment of quiet and some little birds chirped nearby.

"Some of the little birdies can hear you." "Okay! Do another song?!

"And with aloha," he added.

Then he looked at the crowd of familiar faces that had gathered, and prepared to play.

David pronounced, "A-lo-ha."

Sam just finished tuning his guitar, he was sometimes a little sharp, and Frank had his instrument on his lap ready to go.

Many were the times in the singing event of singing in the islands, when the events that had contributed to their thoughts of years gone by were songs in music. These stood one amazed. Some ideals of the long-ago times of the islands were considered, some were well with what was assumed happening.

David, who had prepared for their song playing in public, were all for the considerations of music being played that could have been set in the past. In Honolulu for example around nineteen ten, some of their songs might have been set from before then, but then, it did appreciate good music, it was well written on music paper.

David was practicing at home regularly.

David asked, "Are we planning on playing that ditty?"

"No," his friend replied. "We might try it some other day, but for now, let's just keep doing our originals and let the performers play."

David was as usual, leading their pre-performance song choice. In the conversation on one of their upcoming performances various standards came up.

He asked, "Are we looking at long, long ago times for music, like chants and these are supposed to be re-represented in our songs?"

His friend replied, "Well, there are people doing that. But aren't we looking for cool standards?"

David added, "Thank the performers who brought it through to the present."

Eleven

There were those very long-ago times in the past, those times in the islands when islanders might have known there were some such speculations to consider. They may have supposed there were their Hawaii rulers, these were people who were admired for their healthiness, who were part of a microcosm civilization, who were journeying between the islands. There may be speculation, but speculating about far away islands is historically speculative, a thing that, bordering on the ridiculous, suggests they did, in fact, travel. But then, their return to the islands is supported with the relics of habitats, language developed found in the far distant Pacific islands, and there are scores of dialects. A few or more words correspond throughout many islands.

Of all the islands where more were given an appreciable acceptance, otherwise ruling of the main islands may have been the inclusion of healthfulness. But these may be of some ideals of a time long past, a time valued to the present.

Many of the island groups of the Pacific, there are many islands and atolls to some groups of islands, atolls generally having numerous islands, they come in to comparable size to the islands of Hawai'i, being formed of volcanoes in a much more distant past. It is rather with the recognition of the Hawaiian Islands as a larger group of islands than most of the Pacific island groups that some thought is given to the uniqueness of the Hawaiian Islands.

They had played regularly adding the language variations at times, and this was something the young people listened to and liked. All the people around listening, including those who they hadn't seen for many months, contributed dollars to their hand-woven basket. The patrons took off their hats and plunked down a few dollars, and suggested they play a promotional song.

David added, "I know Lani could hula to this." he thought for a moment, then added, "I think so.", then played the song.

Their next song, which seemed to apply to many travelers, some who might be mariners, adventurers, or explorers who were well among the many people who liked to come and tour. Their next song was soon being heard by the people of the lunch hour, which was about where they played, they were tuned up and had a light, portable P.A. for their set.

David looked about and asked, "" So let's do a landscape song?"

His friend replied, "OK, we are musical artists; we can."

They sat back a second and soon he began strumming down the intro. The accompanying eight verses were supposed to match a number of shells *pupu*.

David mentioned, "Yes! And if you look there at the Pupukea Marine Conservancy there might be an octopus under the wave tops."

He paused for a moment, closed his eyes, and concentrated. Having been to the Pupukea Marine Conservancy, they had been there on really nice days; and he enjoyed sitting on the grass under some Norfolk pine trees near where lava rocks were craggy just by the sea with their miniature canyons, he relaxed. The beach to the side was a treasured location though dangerous when the surf was up. So all that was reminding them of these things was the view from the high, overlooking lookout as of the song. They were about to perform it once more, and they would keep in mind some of these things as well as the nearby religious site. Five hundred feet below that view allowed the overlooking of this area.

The moments passed in the bouncy song, simply.

As they finished this song, they played some other musical instruments, David had played a Jew's harp; the Hawaiian Jew's Harp went into antiquity. And this allowed some instrumental treatments. The few people that listened and wandered away were quickly replaced by other passers-by. This time as the duo was putting up their instruments, collecting the donations from the basket they paused and looked out across the street to landscaped lots which lay below the setting sun across the streets. The sky, which still had some clouds reflecting it were slightly moving, the colors of orange and yellow somewhat blending in with the pale blue sky told them the day was getting onward.

They were saying goodbyes.

David complimented, "Goodbye."

His friend replied, "Bye."

They were packed up and this allowed them to go to an art show nearby. One of them in a large building lobby had art from numerous local artists. The show included artist's concepts for approaches to animals that had been in Hawaiian antiquity, somewhat taken to include the owl, as a man, lizards, sharks, and pigs. The artist of these artworks had portrayed them well, and beautifully included them humanoid. Frank wandered among the many exhibits, some were famous and included ancient Hawaiian voyaging amongst large swells, another portrayed volcanic redness and lava flows; these were little stories they had heard of.

A tune came to his mind, he thought he might be inspired to imagine Lani dancing, with a lizard step; which he thought would be *kahiko* (Hawaiian- hula, ancient). This part of the art exhibit was more on the ancient side. And another part included hula dancers in modern dress.

David was interested in the lore, a hula demonstration they had accompanying the art exhibit was found to portray ancient hunting rather realistically.

Time came in a few more days and they were well downtown. Tuning the instruments before performing was a good practice and he kept up with it.

David commented, "To help this song explain accurately, I have employed many mentions of the take a step of dance choreography."

"Oh, I see," replied Don.

David was familiar with Don's meanderings. David added, "That's nice."

Don Noh replied, "These are sort of to mimic the lizard's movements, with sharp movements."

David laid his ukulele on his lap and rhythmically patted on the ukulele's back as a drum, as nearby Honey, Lani and Fanny were hula dancing, their hands portraying the story of a lizard's picking at an insect, one of its foods.

Another of the songs, and their hula dance told the story of a large fish caught by a fisherman in a canoe.

The song ended and there was a pause that followed.

As bystanders placed a few dollars into their basket, one chuckled and walked off, thinking that the music circled back, to refrains they had played before.

Lani came by. She drove past them and slowed to a stop.

She offered a ride to Fanny.

Fanny was home in about a twenty-minute drive. There was some traffic.

Lani asked "If you return to their performance, I'll be parked nearby, they will pick up their hula friend Honey, and they could appear with David before they had put away their ukuleles."

Don Noh, Fanny, and Honey, who had happened by, were noticed, and Lani had stopped to pick them up in her car. They were at the bus stop.

Fanny said, "We have our billfolds out and actually donate dollars to David E."

David commented, "Do you remember a couple years ago, Honey and Fanny were dancing to a song?"

This was a binding friendship coterie.

Don Noh and Fanny were a few who had smiles to where they would get out of the cab and visit David. Fanny loved to hula, and had been near the venue a few times, when the songbirds were there singing, recalled.

Fanny said, "They were playing, David. You're the compassionate songster they are, and they considered the past, they were talking, and in generous contributions of funds; they were getting especially generous in putting dollars in the basket.

And they were really up on their personalities, the queen, Liliuokalani was who they thought of; imagine her songwriting.

Then there were the times of the hundred to hundred fifty years past, the songs of her reign, which was continuing after David Kalakaua had done his songs, it was well there. There were a lot of perused, and used publicly, original songs. It was quiet that evening."

The scene was reduced; by the thought that the hula's *kumu hula* (Hawaiian- hula teacher), who happened to be passing by, was walking by where they were set up and singing.

Fanny commented, "You're right on, there, David E."

"You are great, too, Fanny," David replied.

Many goodbyes from the many lei venue's shuttered windows sparked. Imagined folk, musicians and dancers, who through topics of the tropics, supported and extended their island story.

A songwriter suggests:, "With singing experience, that is with a lei, it's good to go to locations and musical events; some friendships will develop."

They sang in public parks, and other locations of the town; they sang on flowers, leis, hula dancing, Hawaiian legendary things; and also, exploring Hawaiian language, as well as the sea and surf.

It was soon the Christmas season again, and they sang all the songs for it.

David could add to their holiday repertoire when they were asked to. But it was around and they could sing along.

They knew his short string of holiday standards, including some quite localized, Hawaiian versions, and others.

The season allowed them to explore the holidays and reevaluate their repertoire and include some country folk songs.